nickelodeon

THE LEGEND OF CAPITÁN CALAVERA

By Melissa Lagonegro

Based on the episode "The Legend of Capitán Calavera" by
Leslie Valdes and Valerie Walsh Valdes

Illustrated by Wedoo Studio

A Random House PICTUREBACK® Book

Random House 🏠 New York

rhcbooks.com
ISBN 978-0-593-17272-8 (trade)
Printed in the United States of America
10 9 8 7 6 5 4 3 2 1

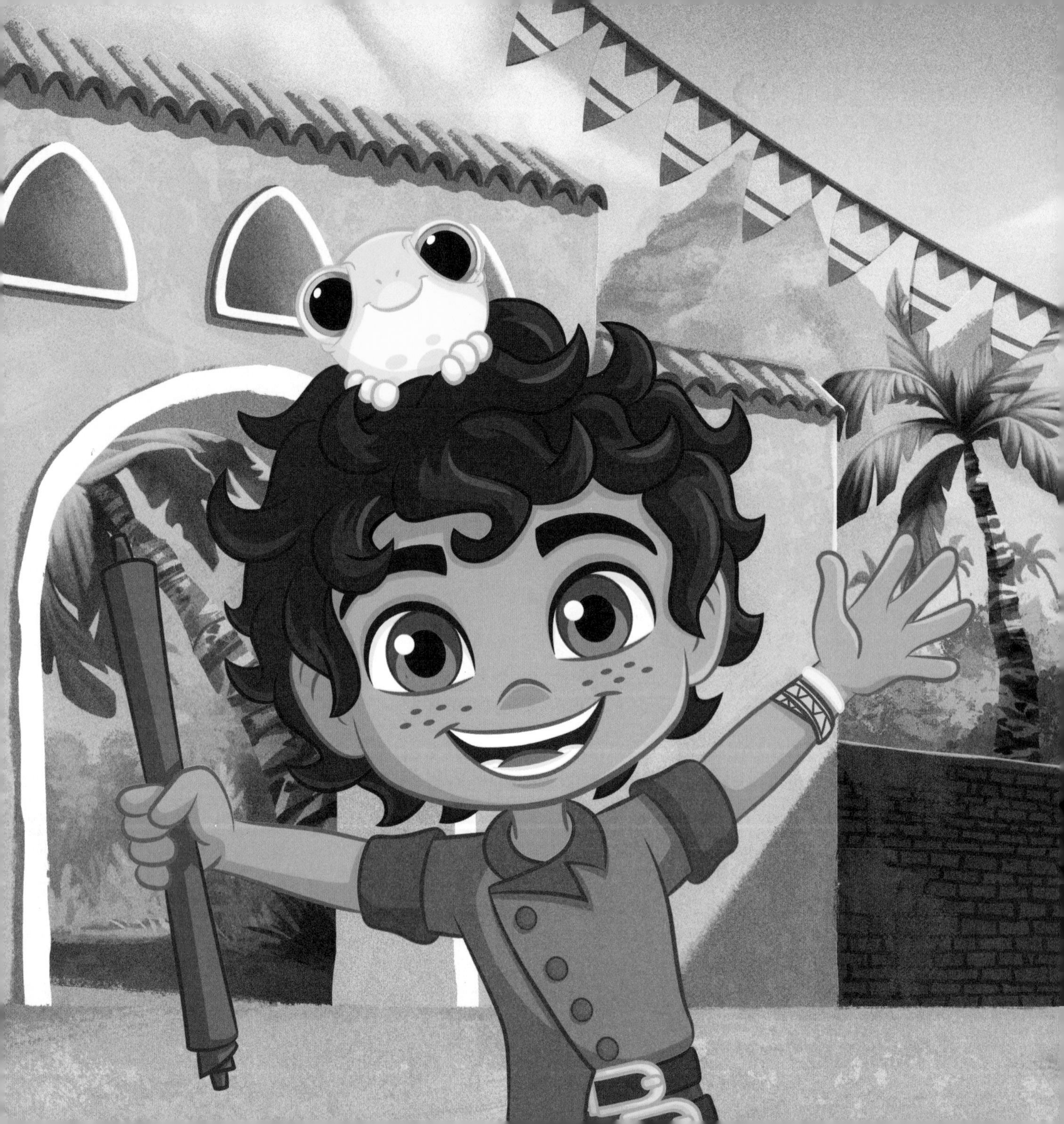

It was a beautiful day on Isla Encanto. Santiago and the people of the island were getting ready for the pirate fiesta!

Santiago spotted his grandpa near a statue he had built.

"Capitán Calavera! He's my hero!" exclaimed Santiago. Capitán Calavera was a good pirate who'd kept the island safe with his enchanted pirate ship. He'd even had a little coquí frog—just like Santiago's frog, Kiko!

"Legend has it that today, on Capitán Calavera's one hundredth birthday, a young pirate will find his long-lost treasure and become the island's new Pirate Protector!" said Abuelo.

"Abuelo, I'm going to find the Calavera Treasure and return it to the people of Isla Encanto!" exclaimed Santiago.

Santiago set off in search of the treasure with the help of his cousin Tomás. Tomás had made Santiago his very own pirate hat. "Now I really feel like a pirate!" declared Santiago. *"Arrr!"*

Just then, Tomás lost his balance and slipped off the edge of a cliff!

"A good pirate helps friends in need!" exclaimed Santiago. He grabbed Tomás's hand—but then they both began to fall!

Magically, a flower quickly grew from the ground. Santiago grabbed the flower and used it to pull them both to safety.

Suddenly, a gust of wind blew Santiago's hat off his head and right into the ocean . . . with Kiko on it!

Santiago jumped into the water. As he swam, a pirate vest appeared on his body and began to glow on Santiago's chest!

"A good pirate never gives up!" declared Santiago. Then a small magical wave carried Santiago right to his little friend.

Safely back on land, Santiago noticed some crabs forming an X on the sand.

"X always marks the spot," said Santiago.

It was Capitán Calavera's treasure!

In the treasure chest, Santiago found Capitán Calavera's Magic Compass. The compass could point the way not only to treasure, but also to any friends in need.

Suddenly, they heard a voice in the distance. "Yo-ho-ho, hee-hee-hee! That there treasure is all for . . .

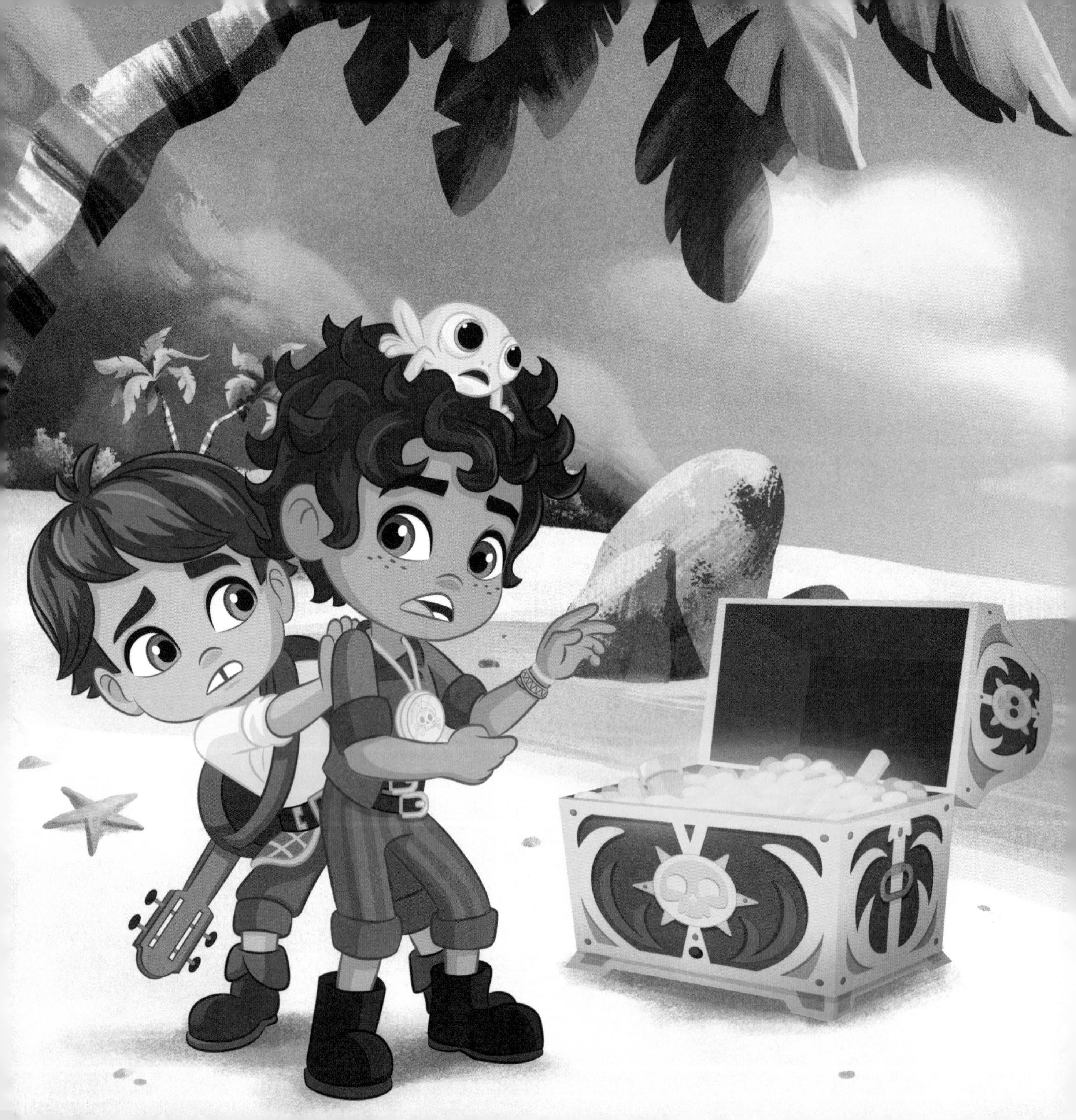

"... ME!"

It was Bonnie Bones, the greediest pirate to ever sail the seas!

"Can it be? The Calavera Treasure?" she asked excitedly. Her mischief-making Kitty Cat Crew grabbed the treasure chest and took it back to their ship!

"We've got to stop her!" shouted Santiago. "Only a good pirate deserves the Calavera Treasure!"

Suddenly, the Magic Compass began to glow. Capitán Calavera's pirate ship, *El Bravo,* emerged from the water!

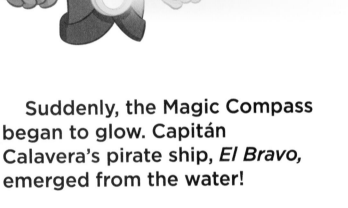

Santiago hopped aboard the pirate ship and instantly transformed into a real pirate! "Blow me down! I'm wearing Capitán Calavera's pirate clothes! *¡Qué maravilla!*" Santiago was the new Pirate Protector of Isla Encanto!

Tomás joined Santiago aboard *El Bravo*. He transformed into Santiago's First Mate! *"¡Adelante!"* Santiago cried, and *El Bravo* sailed straight ahead. Bonnie fired gooey balls of slime at them. *El Bravo* was stuck in the slime!

Santiago called for help from his mermaid friend, Lorelai. Riding a marlin, Lorelai freed *El Bravo* from all the gooey slime. Santiago invited Lorelai to join his crew.

"Aye, aye, *capitán*!" Lorelai replied happily. She used her bracelet of pearl and turned from a mermaid to a girl!

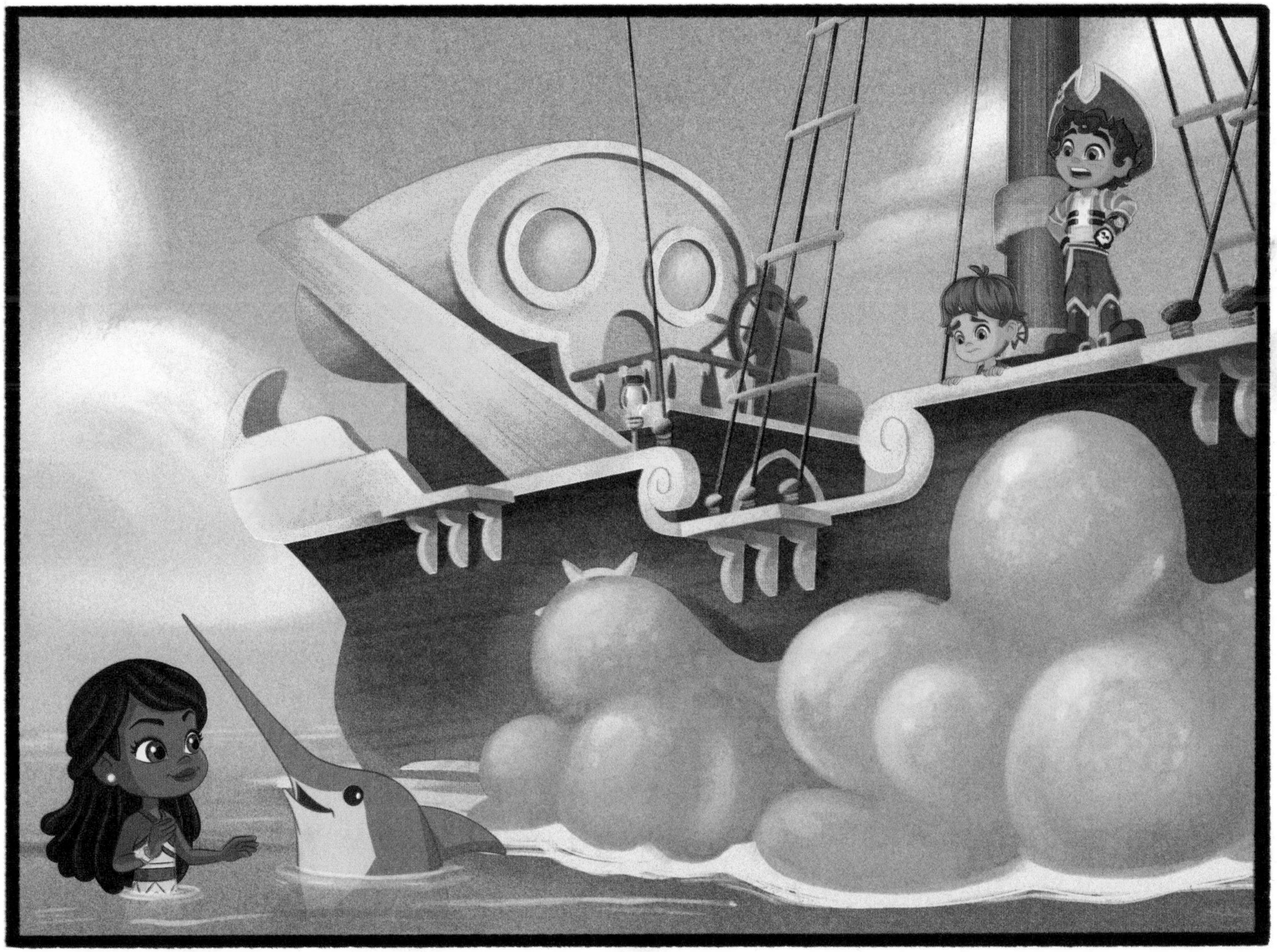

"¡Bravo, rápido!" Santiago commanded.
They quickly caught up with Bonnie.
   Santiago swung onto Bonnie's ship.
"We're here to take this treasure back!"
he exclaimed.
   Capitán Calavera's sword appeared in
Santiago's hand! Santiago used it to wrap
a rope around Bonnie and trap her.

But Bonnie had another trick up her sleeve. She grabbed Kiko! She told Santiago that she would give the frog back in exchange for the treasure and *El Bravo*!

"A good pirate always stands by his matey," Santiago said proudly. "I'll trade you everything for Kiko."

But the sneaky Bonnie Bones took *El Bravo,* the treasure, and Kiko! She'd tricked Santiago again!

"*¡Bravo, abajo!*" he cried. *El Bravo* nosed down into the ocean. Lorelai turned back into a mermaid and called her shark friends to surround the ship. Panicking, Bonnie slipped and dropped Kiko. But Santiago swung over and caught Bonnie, while Tomás saved Kiko!

Santiago got back *El Bravo,* the treasure, AND Kiko! His plan had worked because he was a good pirate who stood by his mateys—just like his hero, Capitán Calavera!

"This isn't the last you'll see of me!" Bonnie shouted as she sailed off.

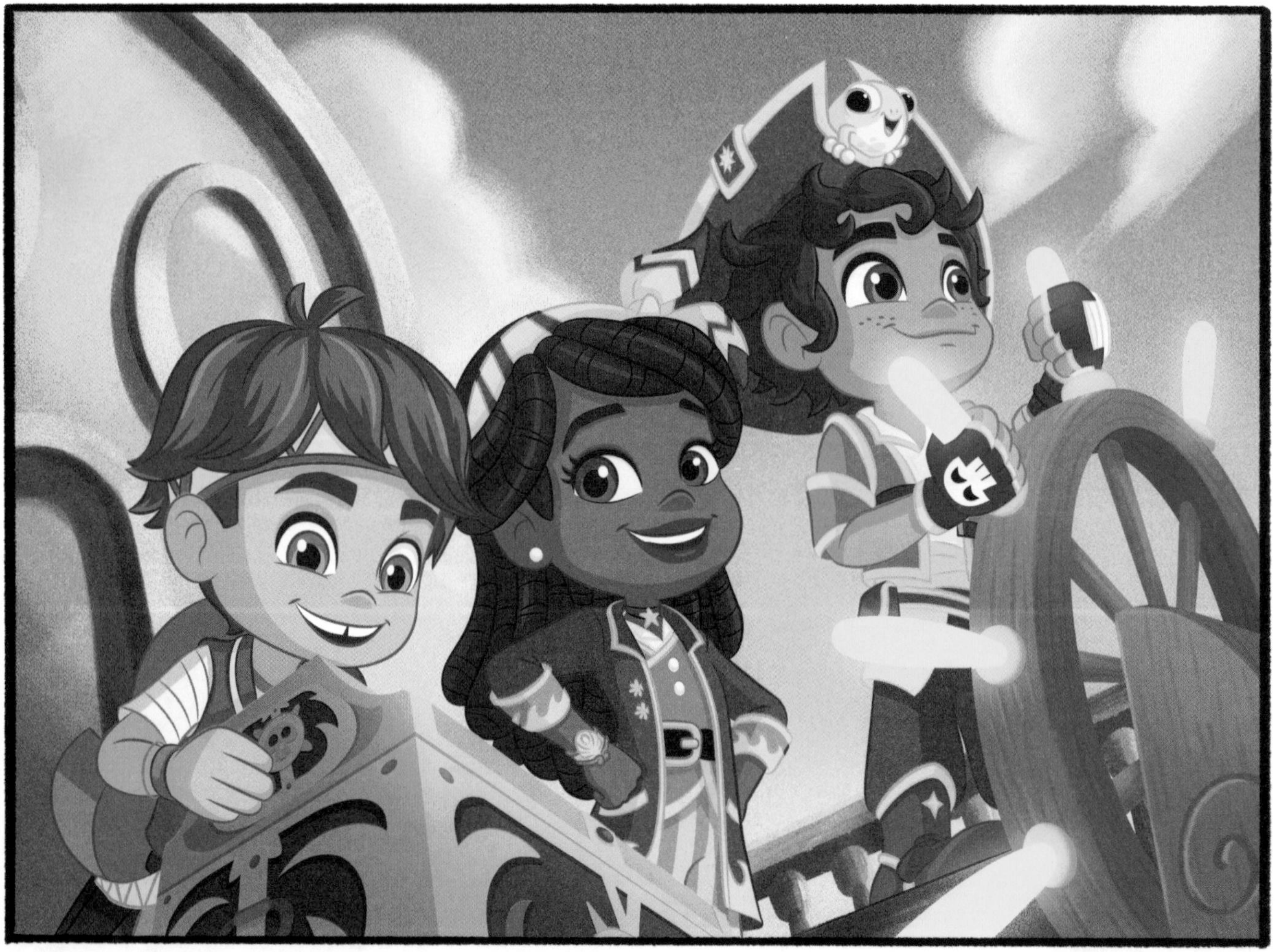

Santiago, Tomás, and Lorelai returned
home with Capitán Calavera's treasure!
"You are now the Pirate Protector of
Isla Encanto!" declared Santiago's *mami*.
She gave Capitán Calavera's special
journal to her son so he could record
all his pirate adventures.

Santiago and the crew couldn't wait to go on more swashbuckling adventures and sail the high seas. *Piratas* ahoy!